BOOKJOY WORDJOY

poems by **Pat Mora**

illustrations by **Raul Colón**

Lee & Low Books Inc.   New York

For Bonny, our treasure —*P.M.*

For Rylie Jade, beautiful dream child,
dream joy —*R.C.*

Acknowledgments

Versions of these poems previously appeared as follows, all poems copyright © by Pat Mora: "Antelope Canyon," *Book of Nature Poetry*, edited by J. Patrick Lewis, 2015; "Bookjoy Around the World," IBBY/USBBY poster, 2011; "Books and Me," Texas Book Festival insert, *Austin American-Statesman*, October 1999; "Happy Visits," *One Minute till Bedtime*, poems selected by Kenn Nesbitt, 2016; "Jazzy Duet/*Dueto de jazz*," Children's Book Council bookmark, 2002; "Library Magic," Tomás Rivera bookmark, 2005, produced in conjunction with Maricopa County, Arizona, Library District stage adaptation of the book *Tomás and the Library Lady* by Pat Mora; "Who's Inside," in "Why Make Poetry a Priority?," *Poetry Aloud Here: Sharing Poetry with Children* by Sylvia M. Vardell, 2014.

My deep thanks to my fine editor, Louise May, and to the gifted Raul Colón. —*P.M.*

LEE & LOW BOOKS INC., 95 Madison Avenue, New York, NY 10016, leeandlow.com
Edited by Louise E. May
Designed by Christy Hale
Production by The Kids at Our House
The text is set in Cantoria
The illustrations are rendered in watercolors and Prismacolor pencils
Manufactured in China by Jade Productions
Printed on paper from responsible sources
10 9 8 7 6 5 4 3 2 1
First Edition
Library of Congress Cataloging-in-Publication Data
Names: Mora, Pat, author. | Colón, Raul, illustrator.
Title: Bookjoy, wordjoy / Pat Mora ; illustrated by Raul Colón.
Description: First edition. | New York : Lee & Low Books, 2018. |
Summary: "A collection of the author's own poems celebrating a love of
words and all the ways we use and interact with them: reading, speaking,
writing, singing, and storytelling."—Provided by publisher.
Identifiers: LCCN 2017051926 | ISBN 9781620142868 (hardcover)
Classification: LCC PS3563.O73 A6 2018 | DDC 811/.54—dc23
LC record available at https://lccn.loc.gov/2017051926

Welcome

Dear Friends,

   I like poems. I like to read them, write them, and gather them together as a gift. This book is my present to you about *bookjoy*, the fun of reading, and about *wordjoy*, the fun of listening to words, combining words, and playing with words—the fun of writing.

   Do you know the word *unique*? It means one of a kind, special. Each of us is unique. In the whole world, there is no one else who is just like you. No one sees a tree just the way you see it or hears the wind just the way you hear it. So no one can write exactly what you can write—if you listen to your inside self and relax in wordplay.

   I hope you enjoy these poems and that you read them again and again. I also hope you read other books of poems and that you write your own poems too—funny poems, scary poems, nature poems, science poems, musical poems, and more. Enjoy sharing them everywhere—at home, at school, at the library, and outside.

   Let's read, let's write, let's explore galore!

—*Pat Mora*

Books and Me

We belong
together,
books and me,
like toast and jelly
o queso y tortillas.
Delicious! *¡Delicioso!*
Like flowers and bees,
birds and trees,
books and me.

Collecting Words

All day, I collect words,
words that move, like *wiggle*,
glowing words, *candle*,
drifting words, *butterfly*,
singing words, *ding-dong*.

I collect words that make me smile, like *tiny*,
that fill my mouth, *bubble* and *bumblebee*,
that float along, *river*,
that have a brown scent, *cinnamon*,
that sweetly stretch, *car-a-mel*.

I collect short, hard words, like *brick*,
soft words, *lullaby*,
cozy words, *snug*,
funny words, *rambunctious*,
scary words, *sssssssssssssnake*,
jumpy words, *hic-cup*,
big words, *onomatopoeia—oink, oink*.

I whisper, say, shout,
        write, and sing my words.

What words will you collect today?

Fireflies

Small gleams of light rise
from sweet, hot grass,
    green, silent *blink*, *blink*,
there, *blink*, and there,
low in bushes, high
    in swaying branches.

Are they lanterns
held by sprites
    who tumble, ride
the evening breeze,
    or tiny twinkles sailing
through our night teasing us
    to dash outside
        and join the darting sparks?

Happy Visits

Cita and I like cookies,
Cita and I like tea.

Cito and I like whistling,
and inventing chocolate recipes.

The three of us like spying
a bunny under a pine tree.

The three of us like lizards
and yellow columbine.

I like to read us stories.
I sit in the middle of us three,

but best of all, best of all, best of all,
I like Cita and Cito to hug me!

We are the hugging three.

Our Cottage in the Woods

I wrote an old-fashioned story, about us, Mama,
about our special cottage in the woods.
Birds play around the plants on the roof.

Mooooooo. Our cow and the sun wake us up.
We milk our cow, pick juicy red berries for breakfast,
and we plant tomatoes in our garden.

We walk on our favorite paths again
making up songs and watching hummingbirds
dip into purple, pink, and yellow wildflowers.

We stir our toes in the cool creek
and then collect blooms to put on our table.
We make delicious cottage vegetable soup.

In the afternoon, we toss apples
to our friends the deer, and we make bread
and read together, smelling, *umm*, our loaf bake.

Our cow sticks her head in the window, saying,
Moooooooo. At sunset, we spread butter
and our homemade berry jam on our warm bread.

We tell stories and hear the wind, *woooooooo*, sing her lullaby.
We snuggle, listening to the wind
whisper *Wooooooooooooooooooooooooooooooo.*

Library Magic

"*¡Vámos!* Let's go to the library!"
Tomás says to his family.
He shows them his favorite books
and his cozy reading nooks.

"*¡Vámos!* Let's go to the library!"
Tomás says to his friends. "Hurry!"
They see *libros* in stacks and rows.
They laugh at funny puppet shows.

¡Vámos! Let's all go to the library!
Join the fun, a treasure house that's free.
Bring your friends and family.
Stories, computers, maps, and more.
Open the magic door.
Like Tomás, savor books and soar.
Be a reader. Explore galore.

Who's Inside?

Are you a lumbering bear inside, *un oso*,
shoving your big ole paw
into a honey hive and licking that gold
sweetness with your thick tongue?

Or are you a cheetah racing
with the wind, running so fast you
                                        fly,
your spots, black streaks?

Are you *una águila*, an eagle screeching,
"*Eeek, eeek,*" over mountaintops,
each wing stretched wide to touch blue
sky, your shiny eyes roaming?

Or are you a giraffe, *una jirafa*,
looking
      down
           down
                down
at us with round, brown eyes
and long, curving lashes?

Listen.
Who's inside your skin?

With your magic wand, draw
your inside self, write
your inside poem, the song
of a bear, a cheetah, an eagle, a giraffe;

or maybe you're a manatee inside,
grazing on grasses all day, all night,
rolling in water all day,
rolling in glimmering white light
      night after night.

Antelope Canyon

For millions of years, water sculpted this sandstone,
      winding and swirling around rocks, waterfalls
buffing sharp corners into curves,
        careening around boulders,
crashing in flash floods, torrents gushing,
       polishing as they roiled and plunged, their force scraping
         smooth canyons and round gold openings,
           sunlight descending in beams,
        columns rising, clouds bursting,
     dark crevices echoing water's roar
       for millions of years.

Dry seasons, streambeds are hushed.
      In winter, snowflakes fall silently into the spirals.
      In spring, snow begins
        its slow melting.
Antelope lick spring stars at sunset.

¡*Bravo!* **Hip-hop Book Day!**

I like Mother's Day
and Father's Day, okay?
Making presents, baking cookies, oh yay!
But April brings our day. *¡Olé!*
Kids and Books Day. *¡Olé!*
¡Bravo! Our hip-hop book day.

Savoring a book buffet,
I become a book gourmet.
Sampling books on display,
I turn the page
and fly away in wordplay.

So why delay?
Why wait to read *some*day?
Let's read books, borrow books, buy books,
make books! Create, eh?
Kids and books every day.
¡Bravo! Our hip-hop book day.
        ¡Olé!

Writing Secrets

I know a secret,
    and it's about you.
Hints for making your writing
    exciting and new.

There's no one like you.
    Know that inside,
then let yourself
    doodle, daydream, imagine.

Think of the faces, the colors,
    the places you've been, the pictures
you carry inside; your hobbies
    and pets, times you were sad,
favorite books, races you ran,
    a splash in a pool,
funny surprises you, only you,
    carry inside.

Now to begin, write your first draft
    and read it to *you*.
What can you add?
    Play with the sounds.
        Try painting with words.

Writers begin again and again.

We have stories to share,
    poems and songs too.
Don't be shy. With a grin,
    share your writing
        with family and friends.

Imagine! Create!
Feel the wordjoy, feel the *zing*
    when you like what you write?

Writers begin again and again.

And we usually know more
    than when we begin.
May what you create
    flip your frowns to a grin.

Singing and Sashaying

When I paint on white paper, I dip
my brush or fingertips and follow
the yellow and green swirls, suddenly see
a parrot on the paper looking at me.

When I sing, I sail
my song into the air,
hear a bird answer my yellow melody.
Inventing, we become a clever pair.

When I dance, my shoulders and
feet feel the beat. I spin, stamp,
try new rhythms as I sashay
    yellow steps down the leaf-covered street.

When I write, I listen,
hear stories and poems inside, repeat
sounds, play with colors and snappy beats.
    I create a great green parrot and me
        singing and sashaying down a yellow street.

Jazzy Duet
Dueto de jazz

Play
> *Juega*

with sounds.
> *con sonidos.*

Improvise!
> *¡Improvisa!*

Slide into a river of music,
> *Resbala a un río de música,*

slish, slosh,
> *rurro, rorro,*

a duet
> *un dueto*

with tree's leafy rhyme,
> *con la frondosa rima del árbol,*

with cricket's castanet clicks,
> *con las castañuelas del grillo,*

with coyote's moon croon.
> *con la copla lunar del coyote.*

Sing too.
> *Canta tú.*

Sing. *Canta.* Sing.
> *Canta.* Sing! *¡Canta!*

Wordjoy

W hy do I like to rhyme,

O pen a special story,

R epeat my favorite words,

D iscover what I can write?

J uggling round, singing sounds,

O yes! It's *música* I hear,

Y ear after wordjoy year.

Bookjoy Around the World

We can read, you and I,
see letters become words
and words become books
we hold in our hands.

We hear whispers
and roaring rivers in the pages,
bears singing
happy tunes to the moon.

We enter spooky gray castles,
and in our hands, flowering trees climb
to the clouds. Bold girls fly;
boys fish for sparkling stars.

You and I read, round and round,
bookjoy around the world.

Note to Educators and Families

I've liked words, rhymes, and books as far back as I can remember. I'm grateful to those who read to me, who encouraged me to read, who expected me to memorize poems (or face a frown), who encouraged me to write, and who for more than thirty years have published my creative work, my wordplay (and wordwork) that led to wordjoy. I spend time with dictionaries and thesauruses. Am I lucky or what?

As a former teacher, I understand and chat with students about the importance of clear expository writing. But this book is about creative writing: wordplay. The hints in the poem "Writing Secrets" are based on suggestions in my book *Zing: Seven Practices for Educators and Students*. It's fun to share what we enjoy, and writing poems for children is one way I hope to share the pleasure of wordjoy, of discovering new words, of listening to words, of hearing them rhyme, of braiding English and Spanish or other languages into a poem, of shaping words on a page. I hope to inspire shining new poets to take risks on the page and to savor that pleasure. Developing the reading/bookjoy habit, of course, is the first secret, but all creative endeavors are a mix of work and play. Too often our young readers and writers experience the work and not the play, the wordjoy. They need strategies, encouragement, and an attentive audience. Together, let's invite beginners of all ages to join our diverse family of readers and writers.

—*Pat Mora*

Heart Music

H ave you watched a child
E xplore the language of love, experimenting,
A rranging the sounds, then the words, the letters, playing,
R earranging in Spanish, Tewa, English, Chinese, Arabic, each
      language lovely, fragrant as flowers, the child
T eaching us—if we'll listen—how to hand someone a bouquet
      of sounds, a heart song, *una canción del corazón.*